A Puppy Impostor!

Nancy didn't get it. A well-trained dog like Sammy would never go wild in the middle of a show. No way!

The curtain came down quickly. Blair McIntyre walked onto the stage in front of the curtain. Her voice cracked as she spoke to the audience. "I'm afraid today's performance is canceled—and all others until we find out what's wrong with our star dog."

Confused whispers filled the theater as the lights came on.

"What happened to Sammy?" Bess wailed.

"You mean if that *was* Sammy," Nancy said.

"Huh?" George asked.

"What if," Nancy said in almost a whisper, "the real Sammy . . . was switched with a fake?"

Join the **CLUE CREW**
& solve these other cases!

NANCY DREW AND THE CLUE CREW®

#38

A Musical Mess

BY CAROLYN KEENE

ILLUSTRATED BY MACKY PAMINTUAN

Aladdin

New York London Toronto Sydney New Delhi

🫖 ALADDIN
An imprint of Simon & Schuster Children's Publishing Division
1230 Avenue of the Americas, New York, NY 10020
First Aladdin paperback edition July 2014
Text copyright © 2014 by Simon & Schuster, Inc.
Illustrations copyright © 2014 by Macky Pamintuan
All rights reserved, including the right of reproduction in whole or in part in any form.
ALADDIN and related logo, NANCY DREW, and NANCY DREW AND THE CLUE CREW are registered trademarks of Simon & Schuster, Inc.
For information about special discounts for bulk purchases, please contact Simon & Schuster Special Sales at 1-866-506-1949 or business@simonandschuster.com.
The Simon & Schuster Speakers Bureau can bring authors to your live event.
For more information or to book an event contact the Simon & Schuster Speakers Bureau at 1-866-248-3049 or visit our website at www.simonspeakers.com.
Book design by Karina Granda
The text of this book was set in ITC Stone Informal.
Manufactured in the United States of America 1219 QVE
10 9 8 7 6 5
Library of Congress Control Number 2013948651
ISBN 978-1-4424-9512-8
ISBN 978-1-4424-9514-2 (eBook)

CONTENTS

CONTENTS

ChaPTER ONE

Unlucky Star

"I declare this Saturday 'Francie Day' in River Heights!" Mayor Strong told the crowd in front of the River Heights Theater.

Eight-year-old Nancy Drew cheered along with Bess Marvin and George Fayne. The girls and the people of River Heights had good reason to celebrate. The national tour of a real live Broadway musical called Francie was in town for two whole weeks!

"This show is practically famous!" Nancy said excitedly. She knew the show was about a farm girl who travels all over the country to find the owner of a lost dog named Sammy.

"I have the CD of the show music," Bess said proudly. "I taught myself all the songs!"

"I hope you taught yourself how to sing, too," George joked.

Nancy giggled as Bess rolled her eyes. Her two best friends are cousins. They are always teasing each other, probably because they are so different.

Bess has blond hair, blue eyes, and a room full of fashion-forward clothes. George, with her dark hair and eyes, likes clothes too—as long as they have tons of pockets for electronic games and computer parts!

"Just think," Nancy said, "we'll get to see the whole show this afternoon—from the front row!"

"Thanks to my mom," George reminded them proudly.

Mrs. Fayne ran her own catering company. Later she would cater a big after-show party for the cast and crew of *Francie* to celebrate opening night.

"And now," Mayor Strong announced as

music from the show blared in the background, "I'd like to introduce the director of the show, Blair McIntyre!"

Nancy smiled as a tall woman with curly black hair stepped forward. Seeing the director was exciting, but the person Nancy really wanted to meet was Kira Swain, the ten-year-old actress who played Francie.

"I want to meet Sammy the dog!" Bess said. "He's the real star of the show."

Nancy gasped as the stage door began to open. Who was coming out next? Was it Kira? Sammy?

"It's just the Star Squad," George, a bit disappointed, said as a bunch of kids filed out the door.

The Star Squad was a summer acting camp in River Heights. This summer they had been asked to play Francie's farm friends in the show.

Nancy recognized some friends from school, like Nadine Nardo, the class actress. There was also Marcy Rubin and her little sister, Cassidy. But who was the kid in the big heavy cow mask?

Her thoughts were interrupted when some-one in the crowd shouted, "Boooooo!"

"Did someone just say 'Boo'?" Nancy asked.

"Maybe the cow said 'Moo,'" Bess suggested.

"I'm pretty sure it was 'Boo,'" Nancy said. "But who could be so mean?"

She got her answer as the girls turned around. Standing behind them was a group of people wearing costumes.

"Booooooooo!" a tall man dressed as a pirate shouted again. The music was too loud for anyone to hear—anyone but Nancy, Bess, and George!

"It's not nice to boo," Nancy told the man.

"Who are you guys, anyway?" George asked.

The pirate puffed out his chest and declared, "I am Winslow Minty, the director of the Croaking Frog Players theater company."

The other actors with him took sweeping bows.

"Are you here to see *Francie*?" Bess asked.

"I should say not!" Winslow scoffed. "We are here because *Francie* has taken over *our* theater!"

"Each summer the Croaking Frog Players performs at the River Heights Theater," an actress wearing a long flowing dress explained. "Because of *Francie*, we have to perform in the old cookie factory!"

Nancy saw that some of the actors were holding up signs that read FRANCIE, GO BACK TO BROADWAY!

"They can't go back now," Nancy said. "The show opens today at three o'clock."

Winslow narrowed his eyes. "Not if I can help it," he muttered. But then he threw back his head and began to sneeze.

The girls stepped back as Winslow sneezed over and over again.

5

"Ahhhh-chooo!" Winslow sneezed. He turned to the actors and said, "We had better leave now. *Ahhh-choooo!"*

Nancy, Bess, and George watched as the Croaking Frog Players quickly left.

"Maybe they should change their name." Bess giggled. "To the Sneezing Frog Players!"

"Who ever heard of a sneezing frog?" someone with a familiar voice asked.

The girls turned to see their friend from school, Shelby Metcalf. But she wasn't alone. Shelby and a college-age girl were grasping the leashes of six dogs.

"Are all those dogs yours, Shelby?" Nancy gasped.

Shelby grinned as she shook her head. "They're from the Rollover Rescue Shelter," she explained. "It's where I'm volunteering this summer."

"Neat!" Nancy said. She noticed that Shelby was wearing a yellow Rollover Rescue T-shirt. So was the girl with her.

The dogs wore yellow scarves around their necks. Each scarf had the words ADOPT ME printed in black letters.

"I read online that Sammy was adopted from a shelter," George said.

"You mean Sammy, the *star* dog?" Shelby asked.

"I also read that Sammy has his own dressing room with a canopy doggy bed," George went on, "crystal treat jars, and a flat-screen TV for watching dog movies."

"I didn't know that," Nancy admitted.

Shelby's eyes grew wide as she said, "Neither did I!"

The crowd suddenly went wild as Kira Swain burst from the stage door. She was wearing Francie's famous blond wig and blue dress.

"It's Kira!" Nancy gasped.

"Hi, everybody!" Kira told the crowd. "And let's give a Broadway bark for my four-legged friend and costar, Sammy!"

Bess cheered so loudly, Nancy had to cover her

ears—especially as the sandy-colored Airedale terrier ran to Kira's side. Holding Sammy's leash was a short man with dark hair.

"That's Sammy's trainer, Carlos Arroyo," Nancy said. "I saw a picture of him and Sammy in my dad's newspaper."

A few of Shelby's shelter dogs began to bark. Carlos frowned as his eyes searched the audience.

"Uh-oh." Shelby sighed. "I'd better go before these dogs upset the diva dog."

Nancy said a quick good-bye to Shelby, and then she, Bess, and George squeezed through the crowd toward Kira and Sammy. As the girls got closer Nancy noticed a white mark on Sammy's front leg. It was shaped like a star!

A star for a star! Nancy thought.

Mayor Strong handed Kira a microphone. She smiled as she began singing the hit song from the show: "I Never Give Up." Sammy got into the act too, jumping up and licking her face at just the right moments.

For the big finish, Kira sang the last words of the song, then kneeled down next to Sammy, who howled along with her last note before licking her again.

"I may like dogs," Bess said as they clapped, "but dog spit is way gross."

When the song was over, Kira traded her microphone for a pen.

"Kira will now sign a few autographs," Mayor Strong announced. "Sammy has already signed a few pawtographs!"

Carlos held up a piece of paper. On it was a black print of Sammy's paw.

"I want one of those!" Bess said.

The girls were about to line up for autographs and pawtographs when—

"Eeeeeeeek!!!"

The earsplitting scream came from Kira, who was shrieking as ink from her pen gushed up in her face!

"Heeeeeeelp!!!" Kira sputtered. "Make it stop! Make it stooooooop!!!"

CHAPTER TWO

Sammy Whammy

Kira looked horrified as she dropped the still-squirting pen. Her snowy-white collar was now stained blue!

"All I did was press down on the pen to write," Kira cried. "And it squirted me!"

Nancy frowned. She had seen that trick pen before. And it was bad news!

"Oh no, Kira!" Blair cried. "Your costume is ruined!"

"So is my *face!*" Kira cried.

"No, it's not!" Nancy blurted out.

All eyes turned to Nancy.

"That pen is from Gordy's Gag Shop on Main Street," Nancy explained. "The ink will disappear in an hour."

"Um . . . two hours," a muffled voice called out.

"Who said that?" Mayor Strong asked.

The kid in the cow suit lifted his mask. When the girls saw who it was, they groaned. It was Antonio Elefano—the class pest!

"The ink will disappear in two hours," Antonio said with a grin. "Two hours and seven minutes, to be exact."

"How do you know so much about this pen, Antonio?" Blair demanded. "Did you give it to Kira?"

Antonio didn't answer, but little Cassidy Rubin stepped forward. She was wearing farm-style overalls and a checkered shirt.

"Antonio didn't give the pen to Kira," Cassidy said. "I saw him sneak it into her dressing room when she wasn't there!"

"Put a sock in it, Cassidy!" Antonio hissed.

But it was too late. . . .

"Antonio Elefano," Blair said coldly. "I'd like to speak to you in private, please."

"He's in trouble," George whispered.

"It's about time," Nancy whispered back.

Kira began crying as she ran back into the theater.

Mayor Strong cleared his throat nervously, then told the crowd, "I'm sorry, but there'll be no autographs. We'll see you later at the show."

Disappointed groans filled the air. Carlos turned as he led Sammy toward the stage door.

"Wait, Mr. Arroyo, wait!" Bess called as the girls raced forward. "Can I get Sammy's pawto-graph? Please?"

"Yes, but just one," Carlos said. He handed Bess a pawtograph, then walked Sammy through a separate door. A star-shaped sign on the door read SAMMY.

"A private dressing room too," George said. "Not too shabby for a dog!"

"A *star* dog," Bess added. She smiled at the

paw on the paper. "And I have his pawtograph!"

"Let's hope *that* ink doesn't disappear!" Nancy said with a smile.

Bess slid the pawtograph into her backpack. She glanced at her watch and said, "It's already noon, and the show is in three hours."

"So?" George asked.

"So I want to go home and change into my theater outfit!" Bess said. "Don't you?"

George nodded down at her T-shirt and jeans. "This *is* my theater outfit!" she said as Bess rolled her eyes.

The girls decided to walk home through the park. The trees were thick with dark-green leaves. Kids and grown-ups were doing summery things like eating ice cream, sitting on the grass, and riding bikes and skateboards.

"Hey, check it out!" George suddenly said.

Nancy and Bess stopped to look where George was pointing. In the distance was a colorful contraption filled with hoops, jumping bars, climbing frames, and a tunnel.

"Is that a new playground?" Nancy asked.

A girl up ahead turned and smiled. It was Mia Murphy from the fourth grade. The kids at school called her Mia Trophy because of all the awards she liked to win.

"It's not a playground," Mia said, walking over. "It's a canine agility course."

"A what?" Bess asked.

"It's like an obstacle course for dogs," Mia explained. "And it's all part of the Doggy Summer Games in two days. I read about it and wanted to check it out."

Nancy liked the idea of the Doggy Summer Games, even though her own puppy was much too young. Chocolate Chip's favorite games were still belly rubs and chasing squirrels!

"You have a new dog, right?" Nancy said. "Are you entering him in the games?"

"I guess you haven't met Ralph." Mia snorted. "The only game he would win is a chewing or howling contest!" She sighed as she gazed at the agility course. "I like Ralph, but I wish I had a pet good enough to enter in the games."

"Then what you need is a star dog," George said.

"A star dog?" Mia repeated.

"A dog like Sammy, from the show *Francie*," George said.

"Sammy would probably win that agility course in a blink!" Nancy agreed.

"Win, huh?" Mia said, almost to herself. "Then *that's* what I need—a star dog!"

As the girls walked away George whispered, "As if Carlos would ever lend Sammy to anyone."

"Speaking of Sammy, we'd better hurry home," Nancy said excitedly. "It's almost show-time!"

Nancy, Bess, and George left the park and headed for their houses. They each had to follow the same rule: They could walk anywhere as long as it was fewer than five blocks from home and as long as they were together.

Once home, Nancy took a cool bubble bath,

then put on her favorite summer dress for the show.

At two thirty Mrs. Fayne drove the girls to the River Heights Theater in her catering van. She wanted to get to the theater extra early to deliver the party food.

"Just think," Nancy said outside the theater. "The actors must be putting on their costumes and their makeup."

"I wonder if Sammy wears makeup," Bess said.

"Give me a break, Bess," George said. "Dogs don't wear . . ."

George stopped midsentence as Sammy's dressing room door began to open. Nancy, Bess, and George backed up against the wall as it swung open.

From behind the door, the girls peeked out.

They saw a man dragging what looked like a huge plastic crate out of Sammy's dressing room. The man used his foot to shut the door behind him. He didn't see the girls as he headed to a black car parked behind the catering van.

"That's Winslow Minty," Nancy whispered. "From the Croaking Frog Players."

One of the actresses who was with him earlier helped Winslow put the crate into the car. As Winslow closed the trunk he said in his usual booming voice, "We'd better go, Miranda! I just did a very bad thing!"

Winslow and Miranda hopped into the car. Nancy, Bess, and George watched it zoom off.

"I wonder what was inside that crate," Nancy said. "And what was that bad thing Winslow was talking about?"

There was no time to talk about Winslow or the crate. The heavy double doors to the theater swung open, and two young men in dark-red uniforms stepped out.

"Tickets, please!" one announced.

"OMG!" Bess squealed. "This is it!"

Mrs. Fayne hurried over with the tickets. Nancy, Bess, and George followed her into the theater, where an usher led them to their seats in the very front row!

"Can we get popcorn?" George asked.

Bess groaned and said, "This isn't a movie theater, George, it's a theater for plays, and that means no popcorn!"

"Enjoy the show," the usher said, after handing them each a *Francie* program.

"Oh, we will!" Nancy said brightly.

The front row was right behind the orchestra pit. Below were musicians tuning their instruments. There were violins, horns, flutes—even a harp!

Nancy couldn't believe it. Was she really at a

Broadway show right in River Heights?

The lights dimmed. The orchestra began playing music.

"This is called the 'overture,'" Mrs. Fayne explained.

Then came the most exciting part of all: The curtain began to rise. The girls gasped when they saw the stage, decorated to look like a farm—haystack and all. Standing onstage was the Star Squad, wearing their costumes.

"There's Antonio in his cow mask," Bess whispered. "He'd better behave."

Nadine recited a few lines. So did Marcy. Then—

"Moo!" the cow bellowed as Kira made her stage entrance with Sammy. Nancy was relieved that the ink stain had disappeared from Francie's dress . . . but her famous wig looked different. Instead of blond curls, it had blond braids!

Kira smiled as she began singing "I Never Give Up."

Nancy smiled too as she waited for Sammy to jump up and lick her face. But this time he didn't. Instead the dog threw back his head and began to howl. And howl. And howl!

Still singing, Kira stared at Sammy, horrified. "I don't think he's supposed to do that," George said.

"Or that!" Nancy said as Sammy started darting back and forth across the stage, barking.

"Sammy, stop!" Carlos shouted as he ran onstage. He tried to grab Sammy, but the dog was already charging head-on into the haystack. The musicians shouted and screamed as hay flew into the orchestra pit!

Nancy didn't get it. A well-trained dog like Sammy would never go wild in the middle of a show. No way!

The curtain came down quickly. Blair McIntyre walked onto the stage in front of the curtain. Her voice cracked as she spoke to the audience. "I'm afraid today's performance is canceled—and all others until we find out what's wrong with our star dog."

Confused whispers filled the theater as the lights came on.

"What happened to Sammy?" Bess wailed.

"You mean if that *was* Sammy," Nancy said.

"Huh?" George asked.

"What if," Nancy said in almost a whisper, "the real Sammy . . . was switched with a fake?"

CHAPTER THREE

Big Break or Big Fake?

"If the show is canceled," Mrs. Fayne sighed, "then so is the after-show party."

The girls talked quietly as they followed Mrs. Fayne backstage.

"What do you mean, a fake, Nancy?" Bess whispered.

"He looked like the real Sammy to me!" George said.

"He may have looked like Sammy," Nancy whispered, "but he sure didn't act like him."

Backstage was just as wild as onstage. Nadine shrieked as the dog chomped through Mrs. Fayne's fruit platter. Marcy and Cassidy were there too, trying to pull Sammy away from the table.

"He's out of control!" Marcy shouted.

The dog was now leaping at a creamy strawberry shortcake. One of his paws was covered with strawberry jam!

"What a mess!" Kira began to sob. "First my wig goes missing, and now Sammy goes bonkers!"

"I don't know what's gotten into him," Carlos said as he ran toward the dog. "He was fine all morning."

"I told you to have an understudy for Sammy," Blair said. "Another dog to take his place in an emergency."

Carlos grabbed the dog's collar and gently pulled him away from the cake. But when he kneeled down in front of him, his eyes grew wide.

"That's strange," Carlos said, looking the dog up and down. "There's no star-shaped mark on his front leg. His fur isn't clipped as short either—"

"Carlos, what are you saying?" Blair cut in.

"I'm saying this dog is not Sammy!" Carlos insisted.

Nancy looked at Bess and George as if to say, *I told you!*

"Not Sammy?" Kira cried.

"If that isn't the real Sammy," Blair said, "then where *is* the real Sammy?"

Carlos slowly shook his head. "I—I don't know!" he stammered.

The dog broke away from Carlos and ran in the direction of the girls. He jumped up on George, his paws landing on her chest.

"Down!" Carlos said, tugging the dog off George.

"Ew!" Bess said. She pointed to a strawberry paw-print stain on George's T-shirt. "Look what he did to your shirt."

"That's okay." George chuckled. "Now I have a pawtograph too!"

But Blair wasn't laughing. "If our star dog isn't back to normal soon," she said, "we're canceling all performances in River Heights."

Cancel the show? Nancy's heart sank. What if she, Bess, and George never got to see *Francie*? Or any Broadway show? She couldn't let that happen!

"Time to go now, girls," Mrs. Fayne said. She was holding a cardboard box filled with unused party supplies.

"Bess, George," Nancy said softly as they followed Mrs. Fayne out of the theater, "if Sammy *was* switched, maybe there's a way to find the real Sammy!"

"But who would take Sammy?" George asked.

"And switch him with another dog?" Bess added.

Nancy tapped her chin thoughtfully, then said, "I'm not sure yet. But it's time for the Clue Crew to find out!"

"It's too bad you didn't get to see the show, Nancy," Mr. Drew said, taking a dinner roll from the bread basket.

Nancy nodded. She wished she could talk with her mouth full, because all she wanted to do was talk about Sammy!

"The dog went bonkers," Nancy finally said. "I think someone switched the real Sammy with a fake Sammy, Daddy."

Hannah Gruen placed another stuffed pepper on Nancy's plate. "So you, Bess, and George want to find the real Sammy, right?" she asked.

"How did you know, Hannah?" Nancy asked, smiling.

"I've been your housekeeper since you were three years old," Hannah said. "I know everything about you, Nancy Drew!"

"Uh-oh!" Nancy giggled. Hannah was more like a mother to Nancy than a housekeeper. No wonder she knew everything!

"Do you think you know who took the real

Sammy?" Mr. Drew asked.

"Maybe Antonio did it." Nancy shrugged. "He could have stolen Kira's wig and decided to steal Sammy, too."

"That would be very hard," Mr. Drew said.

"Why, Daddy?" Nancy asked. Her father was a lawyer but often thought just like a detective!

"Antonio would need a dog that looked just like Sammy," Mr. Drew said. "Where would he find one so fast?" Nancy gave it some thought. Maybe her dad was right. And if Antonio was at rehearsal all day for the show, how would he have had time to get another dog?

"At least you have a souvenir from the show," Hannah said. She handed Nancy the *Francie* program she had gotten at the theater.

Nancy hadn't looked through it yet. She opened the program and something fell out: a small piece of paper.

"What does it say?" Mr. Drew asked.

Nancy read the paper out loud. "The part of the cow will be played by Tommy Maran."

"So Antonio was *not* at the theater all day," Hannah said. "Maybe he got sick."

"Or maybe," Nancy said, narrowing her eyes, "the director got sick of Antonio!"

The next morning the Clue Crew got right to work on the case. It was a warm summer day, so they decided to make the Drews' picnic table their detective headquarters.

"Thanks for bringing your laptop, George," Bess said.

"No problem," George said as she typed. She had already opened a case file called "Sammy— Real or Fake?"

Nancy's puppy, Chip, sat on the grass at their feet.

"Let's figure out a time line," Nancy suggested.

"Carlos took Sammy in at about noon," George said. "And the show was at three, so—"

"So the switcheroo happened between noon and three!" Nancy pointed to the computer. "Write that down, George!"

"I'm writing, I'm writing," George said, her fingers flying across the keyboard.

Suddenly Bess pointed to George's T-shirt and said, "Ew, George. Is that the same shirt you wore yesterday?"

"So?" George said.

"So it's still got the grubby paw print on it!" Bess cried.

Paw print? Nancy's eyes lit up.

"You guys," Nancy said, "if no two fingerprints are the same, what about paw prints?"

"What do you mean?" George asked.

Nancy pointed to the strawberry print on George's shirt. "All we have to do is compare that one to the real Sammy's paw print," she said.

"And I happen to have his pawtograph!" Bess said with a smile. She reached into her backpack and carefully pulled out the print. "I thought this might come in handy today!"

Nancy took the pawtograph and held it up to the print on George's shirt.

"They don't match!" Bess piped up. "The

paw on George's T-shirt is bigger than Sammy's pawtograph."

"So the Sammys were definitely switched!" Nancy said.

"Now we have to figure out who switched them," George said.

While George began their suspect list, Nancy spoke about Antonio. If he wasn't at rehearsal yesterday, he'd have had plenty of time to find a dog that looked like Sammy.

"You guys!" George said. "Antonio's mom runs a doggy day care center in their backyard."

"How do you know?" Nancy asked.

"My neighbors' dog went there while they were on vacation," George said. "It's called Fetching Friends."

"Maybe there was an Airedale at Fetching Friends!" Nancy said excitedly. "Write Antonio's name down, George!"

When she was done, George asked, "Who else?"

Nancy scrunched her eyebrows together as she thought. Then—a brain click!

"Winslow Minty!" she said, suddenly remembering. "We saw him sneak out of Sammy's dressing room with a crate. Maybe it was a pet carrier."

"But why would Winslow want to take Sammy?" Bess asked.

"Winslow was mad at *Francie* for taking the theater," George pointed out. "He might have switched dogs to ruin the show."

"We also heard him say he did something bad!" Nancy said. "Write that—"

"I am, I am," George said as she added Winslow's name to the list.

"We have two good suspects," Nancy said, leaning down to pet Chip. "So let's get to work!"

Antonio's house was three blocks away, so the girls began with him.

Before they left, George finally agreed to change her shirt. "Much better!" Bess said approvingly.

On the way to Antonio Elfano's house, Bess groaned, "I can't believe we're going to Antonio's house. It's probably rigged with practical jokes."

31

They reached the Elefano house. A colorful sign for Fetching Friends Doggy Day Care stood in the front. An arrow on the sign pointed toward the backyard.

"Let's go," Nancy said in a low voice.

The girls slinked alongside the house to the back. They peeked out from around the house into the yard. It was filled with dogs and doggy playthings: balls, Frisbees, chew toys—even a shallow wading pool.

"There's Antonio," George whispered.

Antonio looked bored as he tossed a Frisbee to a tiny white barking dog. There were all kinds of dogs scampering about. All kinds except an Airedale! The Frisbee soared past the little dog, landing in front of a doghouse. A large tan dog stepped out of the house to sniff the toy, then grabbed it between his teeth and brought it back to Antonio. Nancy and her friends gasped. The dog looked just like Sammy!

"OMG!" Nancy whispered. "It must be Sammy!"

ChaPTER FOUR

Backyard Bluff

"Antonio Elefano, give me that dog!" Nancy shouted as the girls charged into the backyard.

Antonio looked surprised to see Nancy, Bess, and George. "No way!" he shouted back.

The Airedale wore a leash. Antonio reached down to grab it, but George grabbed it first.

"What are you doing here, anyway?" Antonio demanded.

"We think that Sammy was switched with another dog," Nancy said.

"And that this is the real Sammy!" George said, holding the leash tightly.

"Why would I want to switch dogs?" Antonio demanded.

"To be pesty!" Bess said angrily.

A sly grin appeared on Antonio's face. "Pesty, huh?" he said. "You mean like this?"

Antonio turned. He tossed the Frisbee way over the wading pool and shouted, "Go get it, boy!"

The Airedale barked, then broke into a run, pulling his leash—and George!

"Stoooop!" George shouted as the big dog dragged her across the grass.

"George, look out!" Nancy shouted.

Too late! The dog raced through the wading pool, yanking George behind him. The wet dog stopped on the other side to snatch up the Frisbee. Also dripping wet was George. She sat up in the pool, the leash still in her hand.

"It's a good thing it's summer," George snapped.

Antonio laughed meanly. "Now will you let go of that dog—and get lost?" He sneered.

"Not until you tell us where you were yesterday afternoon," Nancy said, "between noon and three o'clock."

"I gave that goofy cow costume back and came home," Antonio explained. "When my mom found out what I did with that pen, she made me work all day with these stinky dogs."

"Grounded all day, huh?" George said.

"Not totally," Antonio said. "My mom let me take the dogs on a field trip to the Sit, Stay Café."

Two dogs started fighting over a chew toy. While Antonio ran to break it up, the girls began to whisper.

"Sit, Stay Café?" George asked. "Is that place for real?"

Nancy nodded and said, "They make the cutest doggy cupcakes. Chip loves going there."

Bess shrieked as the Airedale shook water

from his fur, getting her wet too. As the dog lifted his head Nancy noticed a silver heart-shaped ID around his neck. She lifted it and read it out loud: "Mister Chomps."

"That's his name?" George asked.

"But it's supposed to be Sammy!" Bess said.

An idea suddenly popped into Nancy's head. She turned to George and said, "Drop the leash."

George shrugged and dropped the leash. The dog ran a few feet before Nancy called, "Mister Chomps! Here, Mister Chomps!"

The dog's ears perked up. He stopped running, then turned and ran straight to Nancy!

"This must be Mister Chomps," Nancy said.

"Duh!" Antonio said, walking over. "I told you he wasn't Sammy."

Nancy glanced down at the dog's leg. There was no white star-shaped mark either.

"Now do you believe I didn't switch those dogs?" Antonio asked.

"I guess," Nancy admitted. But as she and

her friends left the Elefano house, they still weren't sure.

"What if Mister Chomps was Sammy's name before he got adopted?" Nancy wondered. "And what if Sammy's white star-shaped mark was covered with dirt? Maybe that's why I couldn't see it."

"How do we know Antonio really went to that doggy café yesterday?" Bess asked.

"Easy. We go to the café and ask!" George said. She shook water out of her wet curls, making Bess shriek again.

The Sit, Stay Café was on Main Street and only two blocks away. It was busy with human and canine customers as the girls stepped inside. Some sat at small tables, while others stood at the counter, buying fancy doggy treats.

Nancy spotted the owner of the café, Rochelle Rottweiler. Rochelle was proud to have the same name as her favorite breed of dog.

"Hi, Ms. Rottweiler," Nancy said. "Was there a boy here yesterday with a whole bunch of dogs?"

Rochelle wiped cupcake cream off her hands,

onto an apron. "Many kids were here with dogs," she said. Her eyes suddenly narrowed. "But one kid must have thought he was a comedian."

"What do you mean?" Nancy asked.

Rochelle reached behind the counter for a paper sign that read NO DOGS ALLOWED!

"No dogs allowed?" Bess asked, confused. "That was put up outside?"

"But this is a dog café!" George said.

"Exactly," Rochelle said, crumpling up the sign. "It must have been a practical joke."

Practical joke? Nancy's eyes widened. Practical jokes meant Antonio Elefano!

"What time was the sign put up?" Nancy asked.

"Probably around two or three o'clock," Rochelle said with a frown. "Right before customers stopped coming in."

"Oh," Nancy said. Antonio *was* at the café at the time of the crime.

The girls thanked Rochelle and left the café. Once outside, Nancy said, "Antonio's excuse checked out. I guess he's not a suspect anymore."

"But he'll *always* be a pest!" Bess insisted.

"Our only suspect now is Winslow Minty," Nancy reminded them, "from the Croaking Frog Players."

"We did see him lugging something that looked like a kennel out of Sammy's dressing room," Bess said. "What if the kennel wasn't empty?"

George's stomach let out a loud growl. She patted it and said, "The only thing empty right now is my stomach!"

"Okay, okay." Nancy giggled. "Let's go for some pizza!"

The Clue Crew walked down Main Street toward their favorite pizza parlor. On the way Bess stopped suddenly and said, "Look!"

Nancy looked to see what Bess was pointing to. It was a flyer for the next Croaking Frog Players show.

"The play is called *Sea Dog on Deck*," Nancy said, reading the flyer out loud.

"Dog?" George asked.

"Their next show stars a dog!" Bess gasped.

"And the only star dog I can think of," Nancy said firmly, "is *Sammy*!"

CHAPTER FIVE

Biggest Fan!

After a quick pizza break the girls hurried straight to the Croaking Frog Players' theater.

"This used to be a cookie factory!" Bess said outside the theater. "Do you think they'll still have cookies?"

"We just had pizza!" Nancy said.

"But we didn't have dessert!" Bess said with a smile.

Luckily, the front door was unlocked. Nancy quietly pulled it open. As they stepped inside they looked around.

"Wow!" George exclaimed.

There were no cookie-making machines

anywhere. Or cookies. Instead there were rows of chairs facing a stage.

"It's a real live theater," Nancy pointed out.

"Yeah, but I can still smell the cookies," Bess said, taking a whiff. "Oatmeal raisin!"

Nancy didn't see any other people, just a winding staircase. "Should we go upstairs?" she asked softly.

"Not until I see the set!" Bess said. She raced to the stage and climbed the few steps leading up to it. Nancy and George traded shrugs, then joined Bess.

"Pretty neat," George said, looking around. The stage was decorated to look just like a ship. There were barrels and rope nets. The backdrop was painted to look like a cloudy sky filled with seagulls.

"Look at that!" Nancy said. She pointed to a huge round machine that looked like a fan. "I've never seen such a big fan in my life."

Suddenly—

"Whooooaaaa!"

Nancy turned to see George on the floor. She had slipped on a clump of sandy-colored hair.

"Are you okay, George?" Nancy asked.

"I think so," George said. She nodded at the clump of hair still on the floor. "But where did that come from?"

"What if the hair is dog hair?" Bess asked. "It *is* the same color as Sammy's!"

"If it is Sammy's hair," Nancy said, "then where is he?"

"Maybe in there!" George said, pointing a few feet away. Nancy followed George's gaze and gasped. It was a big plastic crate exactly like the one they had seen Winslow Minty with. Was it a pet carrier?

The girls circled the crate, checking it out. It didn't have a front opening like most pet carriers. Instead it had a lid on top. A closed lid!

"Winslow wouldn't keep poor Sammy in there, would he?" Bess gulped.

Nancy hoped not. She reached out to open the lid. But then—voices!

"Someone's coming!" Bess gasped.

"If they find us snooping around onstage, they'll make us leave," Nancy whispered. "Then we'll never find Sammy!"

"Let's hide!" George hissed. She nodded at the giant fan and said, "Behind that thing!"

The voices grew louder as the Clue Crew ducked behind the fan. After a few seconds the girls slowly peeked out. Nancy felt Bess squeeze her arm. Standing onstage just a few feet away were . . .

"Pirates!" Bess whispered.

Nancy stared at the pirates as they swaggered back and forth on the stage. The lead pirate wore an eye patch and a bandanna over stringy black hair. He said in a booming voice, "Man the cannon, ye cowardly swags—and blow the man down!"

The pirate drew his sword and raised it high.

Bess gave a little shriek. This time she didn't grab Nancy's arm. Instead she grabbed the back of the fan. Nancy heard a click, then—

WHOOOOOOOOOOOOOSSSSSSSSHHHHHH!

A giant gust of wind exploded from the fan, toward the pirates. Nancy could hear them shout as hats and wigs blew off their heads. Even parts of their costumes were ripped off by the powerful wind!

"Bess, shut it off!" Nancy said.

Bess flicked the switch from side to side. The fan began blowing from side to side too. "I can't!" she cried.

"Give me that!" George said. She flicked the switch down. The fan stopped swerving. It began to sputter, until finally it stopped.

Nancy gulped as she looked at the pirates. Without their hats and wigs she could see who they were. They were Winslow Minty and his actors—and they looked mad!

"Who's there?" Winslow demanded.

The girls stepped out from behind the fan.

"Um . . . it was kind of stuffy in here," Bess said. "We thought we'd turn on the fan—"

"That is not a fan!" Winslow bellowed. "It is a wind machine used to create a storm at sea!"

"Sorry," Nancy said. "But we were looking for Sammy, the dog from *Francie*."

"And you thought you'd find him here?" Winslow demanded. "Why?"

"The name of your play is *Sea Dog on Deck*!" George said, folding her arms across her chest. "How do you explain *that*, Mr. Minty?"

"'Sea dog' means 'pirate,'" Winslow explained. "In pirate talk, that is."

"Oh," George said.

"We also saw you sneak out of Sammy's dressing room with that," Nancy said, walking over to the crate. "A crate big enough to hold . . ." She pulled up the lid and stared inside. "Wigs?"

chaPTER Six

Things Get Hairy

Bess and George looked inside the crate too. Inside were piles of wigs—straight, curly, even multicolored clown wigs!

"The hair I slipped on must have come from one of these wigs," George murmured. "Not Sammy."

Nancy turned to Winslow. "So that's what you were taking out of the theater?" she asked. "A bunch of wigs?"

"The wigs belong to the Croaking Frog Players," Winslow insisted. "They had been in the theater since our last show."

"But . . . we heard you say you did something bad!" Nancy told Winslow.

Bess was busy at the crate, going through the wigs. "These are awesome!" she said. "May we try some on, Mr. Minty?"

"Absolutely not!" Winslow said. "Those wigs wouldn't fit you, anyway."

"This one would," Bess said. She pulled out a blond curly wig and popped it on her head. "See? A perfect fit!"

Nancy stared at the wig. That wasn't just any wig! "That's Francie's wig!" she declared.

"Kira did say it was missing," George said. "But how did it get here?"

Winslow cleared his throat as the girls turned to look at him. "Weelll," he said slowly.

"Oh, go on, Winslow," an actress said. "Tell the girls the truth."

Winslow took a dramatic breath. He then looked at Nancy, Bess, and George, and said, "I was mad at *Francie* for using our theater. So I stole the lead actress's wig."

"Where was it?" Nancy asked.

"On a stand in the makeup room," Winslow said. "No one was in there, so I just grabbed it."

"Yeah, but why did we see you coming out of Sammy's dressing room," George asked, "and not the main door?"

"That used to be my dressing room!" Winslow frowned. "I didn't know they had given it to a dog!"

"If you stole the wig," George said, "you could have stolen Sammy, too."

"Never!" Winslow boomed.

"Why not?" Nancy asked.

"Because I'm allergic to dogs!" Winslow declared. "Why would I want something that makes me miserable?"

Allergic? Nancy shot her friends a glance. Winslow had sneezed like crazy after Shelby's dogs had come over.

"Well?" Winslow asked impatiently.

"I guess we believe you, Mr. Minty," Nancy said. Then she quickly added, "But you really should return Kira's wig."

"Yes!" Bess said as she handed Winslow the wig. "Unless *you* want to play the part of Francie one day!"

Winslow muttered under his breath as he grabbed the wig. The Clue Crew thanked the pirates, then left the cookie-factory-turned-theater.

"Winslow is innocent," Nancy said. "Which means we have one fewer suspect."

"That leaves us with zero," George said. "Zero, zip, zilch!"

"I know." Nancy sighed.

The Clue Crew was back to square one!

"I just thought of something," George said as they walked through the park once again. "What if *Francie* leaves before we find Sammy?"

"That's why we can't give up," Nancy insisted.

"Like Francie's song says!" Bess said. She stopped walking to sing at the top of her lungs, "I neeeeeever giiiiiiiive up!"

"Spare me!" George pleaded.

Bess kept singing until suddenly, out of nowhere, charged a sandy-colored dog. He jumped up on Bess and began licking her face!

"Ew!" Bess cried. "Yuck!"

Nancy couldn't believe her eyes. The big dog licking Bess was an Airedale!

CHAPTER SEVEN

Bark in the Park

"Get him off!" Bess cried. By now she was on the ground, the dog still licking away. "It's sooooo gross!"

Nancy and George reached to grab the dog's leash. The dog stopped licking, turned, then dashed off into a thicket.

"Dog spit!" Bess said as she picked herself up off the ground. "There's nothing yuckier!"

"Deal with it, Bess," George said. Her dark eyes were flashing. "Did you see what kind of dog that was?"

"A gross one," Bess said.

Nancy shook her head and said, "It was a dog just like Sammy. Let's find him!"

The girls looked over the bushes for the mysterious Airedale. All they could see were humans sitting on the grass, playing ball, and buying Popsicles from a cart. The only dog walking by was a tiny Chihuahua with its owner.

"It had to be Sammy!" Nancy insisted. "He did what Sammy does during the song."

"Sing it again, Bess!" George urged. "Maybe he'll come back!"

Bess scowled at George and kept wiping her face.

Nancy wanted to look for the mystery dog more than anything—but then she glanced at her watch. "I have to go home now," she said, "to walk my own dog."

"I'm going home too," Bess said, rubbing her sticky cheek. "To take a shower!"

Nancy hurried home. But before she walked Chip, she told her father all about the dog in the park who looked just like Sammy.

"He even licked Bess's face when she sang 'I Never Give Up,'" Nancy said excitedly. "Do you think that dog was Sammy, Daddy?"

"Many dogs must look like Sammy," Mr. Drew said. He smiled as he handed Chip's leash to Nancy. "But only one dog now needs a walk."

"On it, Daddy!" Nancy smiled back. She gave the leash a gentle tug. "Let's go, Chip!"

"Woof!" Chip barked, wagging her tail.

Nancy walked Chip up and down the block. The puppy wagged her tail as she sniffed at tiny flowers growing along the curb. All Nancy could do was think about Sammy. What if *Francie* was already packing to leave River Heights? What if—

"Beep, beep!" A voice interrupted her thoughts.

Nancy turned to see a girl speeding down the block on her bike. It was Mia "Trophy" Murphy.

Mia slowed down and nodded at Chip. "Is that your dog?" she asked Nancy.

"Yes," Nancy replied. "But you can't borrow

Chip for the dog agility course tomorrow."

Mia laughed out loud. "I don't need Chip for the Doggy Summer Games," she said. "Or anyone else's dog."

"Why not?" Nancy asked, trying to keep Chip away from the bike. "Did you decide to enter your dog, Ralph?"

"Not Ralph," Mia said. "The pet I'm entering is a star. A superstar!"

"A star?" Nancy said. Her eyes popped wide open. George had told Mia she needed a star for the games. A star like Sammy!

"What's his name?" Nancy asked.

"That is top secret for now," Mia said. "All I can tell you is that his name begins with an *S*."

Mia pumped her legs as she pedaled off.

Nancy's heart began to pound faster and faster.

"*S* stands for 'Sammy,' Chip!" she said. She frowned as she watched Mia turn the corner at the end of the block. "It also stands for 'suspect' . . . which Mia Trophy is now!"

ChaPTeR EigHT

Game On!

"If it was Mia who took Sammy," Bess said, "where would she find another Airedale to switch him with?"

"Good question, Bess," Nancy said.

It was a hot, sunny Monday morning—the morning of the Doggy Summer Games. As they walked through the park Nancy told Bess and George all about Mia and her mysterious star pet.

"Maybe Mia switched Sammy with her dog, Ralph," George suggested. "She told us Ralph was a chewer and a howler—just like the dog in the show!"

Nancy, Bess, and George hurried straight to the Doggy Summer Games. Not only was the agility course set up, but so were snack stands, balloon carts, and tables selling dog treats. There were plenty of doggy water dishes around too.

A man and two women sat behind a table, studying notes. Nancy guessed they were the judges. But where was Mia?

The girls watched as owners walked by with their dogs. Some wore T-shirts reading TEAM SPARKY or TEAM RASCAL."

"There she is!" Bess called out. She pointed to Mia lugging a pet carrier. Helping her was a boy of about ten.

"Who's he?" George asked.

"I don't know," Bess said. "He doesn't look like he goes to our school."

Mia and the boy set the kennel on a table near the agility course. They dusted off their hands and high-fived.

"I don't care who that boy is," Nancy said. "I just want to look inside that kennel."

The girls hurried over to Mia.

"Hey, Mia!" Nancy called. "Can we—"

The boy held up his hand and shouted, "Stop!"

"Why?" Bess asked. "We just want to see your pet."

"The star can't be bothered before the event," the boy said, his nose in the air.

"Who made you boss?" George demanded.

"This is Miles," Mia said quickly. "The star's owner."

"Owner?" Nancy asked.

Mia was about to explain when a golden retriever padded over. His tail wagged as he sniffed at the kennel.

From it came a loud "Meeeeoooooowww!"

Nancy, Bess, and George traded stares. Dogs didn't meow. What was up?

While Mia and Miles tried to shoo the dog away, the girls ran to the kennel. Peeking through the wire door, they saw a big orange—

"Cat?" Nancy cried. "Your star pet is a cat?"

"Not just any cat," Mia said. "Simon is the national cat agility champ."

"But this is a contest for dogs!" George said.

"The judges won't mind," Miles said with a shrug. "I hope."

"I want to pet the kitty!" Bess insisted. She opened the kennel door a crack. "If I just squeeze my hand in—"

"Don't!" Miles shouted.

Simon gave a hiss. He squeezed out the kennel door and shot off!

"Thanks a lot, Bess!" Mia snapped. "Now we've lost Simon!"

"No, we haven't!" Miles cried. He jumped up and down, pointing to the agility course. "Look at that cat go!"

Everyone cheered as Simon zipped through the tunnel, leaped over the bar, and jumped through a row of hoops. Miles was there to catch him after he rocketed across the finish line.

"Nailed it!" George cheered.

"He's a star, all right!" Bess declared.

"But definitely not Sammy," Nancy said.

The girls left the park. They were glad Mia wasn't guilty of taking Sammy. They were also glad Simon had aced the agility course.

"But now we have no more suspects," George said. "And we looked everywhere for clues."

Nancy was about to agree when a thought crossed her mind. They had never looked for clues inside Sammy's dressing room.

"We did look everywhere," Nancy said. "Everywhere but the scene of the crime!"

ChaPTER NiNE

Room with a Clue

"You mean Sammy's dressing room?" Bess asked. "How would we get inside?"

"Especially since there's no show in the theater now," George said. "The *Francie* performances were canceled, remember?"

"Let's worry about that when we get there," Nancy said. "But first, let's get there!"

The girls walked the few blocks to Main Street. The *Francie* poster was still hanging on the wall outside the theater. This time it had a red sticker on it that read CANCELED. Were they too late?

The outside door to Sammy's dressing room was locked. Nancy rang the bell on the stage door. After a few seconds a woman wearing a gray guard's uniform opened the door. Embroidered on her jacket was her name: MAXINE.

"Sorry, kids," Maxine said. "There are no *Francie* performances right now."

"We know," Nancy said.

"So why are you here?" Maxine asked.

Nancy shot her friends a worried glance. She hadn't thought of an excuse to get into the theater. Luckily, George did!

"We were at the show the other day," George blurted out. "And I lost something in the theater."

"Tell me what you lost, and I'll look for it," Maxine said with a smile.

"Um, I lost my pet!" George said. "My pet mouse!"

Nancy tried hard not to giggle as Maxine wrinkled her nose.

"It jumped out of my pocket during the show," George went on. "He's gray with—"

"There's no way I'm looking for a mouse," Maxine cut in. She stepped aside. "Go in and look yourselves."

"Thank you!" Nancy said as the girls slipped past Maxine and through the door. Maxine nodded and sat on a stool to read a magazine.

"Okay, we're in," George whispered. "But where's Sammy's dressing room?"

"On the outside it's next to the stage door," Nancy said, figuring it out. "So it's probably near the stage door on the inside."

They walked a few steps down the hall to the first door. Quietly Nancy opened it and they slipped inside.

"Wow!" Nancy gasped when she saw the room.

Inside was a canopied dog bed, crystal treat jars—even a vanity covered with canine grooming products. Glossy pictures of Sammy lined the walls.

"Talk about a pampered pup!" George said.

Bess pointed inside a closet filled with dog coats, booties, and even a few hats. "Sammy has more clothes than I do!"

"Stop looking at the clothes, Bess," Nancy said, "and let's start looking for clues!"

The girls split up to search the room. Nancy looked under the bed and mattress. All she found were some dog hairs and kibble crumbs. George looked inside the portable kennel. There was nothing in it but a fluffy white towel and a rubber squeak toy shaped like a shoe.

Suddenly Bess cried out, "Yucky!"

"What's yucky?" Nancy asked.

"Empty dog food cans." Bess pointed into a small garbage pail. "Carlos must have thrown them out the day of the last show."

Nancy peered inside the garbage pail. She saw the cans Bess was talking about. She then saw something else. . . .

"Is that a yellow scarf?" Nancy asked.

George pulled the yellow cloth out with her pointer finger and thumb. It was stained with dog food. It also had the words ADOPT ME printed on it!

"That's the same scarf Shelby's shelter dogs wore," Nancy said slowly.

"Sammy was once a shelter dog," George

said, still holding the scarf. "But that was a long time ago."

"Throw it back in the garbage, George," Bess said, squeezing her nose. "It smells just as bad as the—"

"Wait!" Nancy said. "That might be a clue!"

"A grubby scarf?" Bess asked.

"What if the dog that was switched with Sammy is a shelter dog?" Nancy asked. "One of Shelby's shelter dogs!"

"They did wear yellow 'Adopt Me' scarves," George said. "But why would Shelby want to put a shelter dog in Sammy's place?"

"I don't know," Nancy said. "But if she did, Sammy might be at Rollover Rescue!"

The girls left through the front door and headed straight to the shelter.

A man wearing a yellow Rollover Rescue T-shirt greeted them at the door. Nestled in his arm was a tiny Chihuahua with huge ears and eyes.

"My name is Roy, and this is Genghis," he said, introducing the dog. "Are you girls interested in adopting a pet?"

"We all love animals!" Nancy said, smiling at the Chihuahua. "May we look at some more dogs, please?"

Roy nodded. He pointed in the direction of the playroom. "There'll be volunteers inside to help you," he said. "Good luck."

The girls hurried into a big sunny room filled with dogs and other volunteers. There were all kinds of dogs, chasing balls and taking naps—but no Airedale like Sammy!

Nancy kept looking and looking until—

"What are you doing here?"

Whirling around, Nancy saw Shelby. She was holding the leashes of four dogs she had just walked. One was an Airedale. He did not have a yellow ADOPT ME scarf, but he did have a white star-shaped mark on his leg!

"Okay, Shelby," Nancy said, pointing to the Airedale. "What are you doing with Sammy?"

CHAPTER TEN

Curtain Up!

"Sammy?" Shelby cried. "His name isn't Sammy—it's Knuckles!"

"Knuckles?" Nancy repeated.

"I don't believe it," George said.

"Wait!" Bess said. "There is a way to find out."

"How?" Nancy asked.

"I don't want to do it," Bess sighed. "But . . ."

She threw back her head and began singing "I Never Give Up." With a woof, the dog broke away from Shelby and jumped up on Bess.

"Okay, okay, I proved my point!" Bess cried as the dog licked her face. "Now get him off!"

Nancy gently pulled the dog off Bess. Shelby's shoulders dropped as she muttered, "Rats."

"Come on, Shelby," George said. "We know that dog is Sammy."

"Why don't you just tell the truth?" Nancy asked. "We are your friends, right? And friends don't lie to friends."

Shelby blinked back tears. She let go of the other three leashes so the dogs could play.

"That is Sammy," Shelby admitted. "The dog you saw in the show is Knuckles . . . a shelter dog."

"So you did switch Sammy with a shelter dog!" Nancy said. "Why?"

"When you told me about Sammy's fancy

life, I felt sorry for Knuckles," Shelby explained. "He wasn't getting adopted by anyone."

"Poor Knuckles," Bess said sadly.

"I wanted Knuckles to feel like a star—even for just a day or two," Shelby said. "So before the show I snuck into Sammy's dressing room and switched dogs!"

Shelby explained how she'd snuck in through the front door while Sammy was resting on his bed. She'd put Knuckles on the bed and walked Sammy out the door.

"I threw away Knuckles's 'Adopt Me' scarf before I left," Shelby added, "so nobody would know he was really a shelter dog."

"Why didn't you put a scarf on the real Sammy?" Bess asked, nodding at the dog.

"Because I didn't want anyone to adopt the real Sammy," Shelby said, wide-eyed. "Then I'd really be in trouble."

"I don't think you'd be in trouble for telling the truth." Nancy shrugged. "The director of *Francie* would want to know what happened."

"But they'd hate me for spoiling the show!" Shelby wailed. "I thought since Knuckles looked like Sammy, he'd act like Sammy too. How did I know he didn't like music?"

"Or Broadway show tunes." George shrugged.

"I'm sure they just want Sammy back, Shelby," Nancy said, smiling at the dog. "The real Sammy."

Shelby seemed to think about it. She finally turned to Sammy and said, "Come on, boy. You're going home."

Nancy was right. Blair McIntyre was so happy to see Sammy that she accepted Shelby's apology. Sammy was so happy to see Kira again that he licked her face without even hearing the song!

The Clue Crew's case was finally closed. And only two days later, Nancy, Bess, and George got to celebrate the reopening of *Francie* in the same great seats!

"I'm glad Sammy's home," Bess said.

"Even Knuckles found a home," George reminded them. "That lucky dog was adopted by Carlos."

Nancy nodded and said, "Now Carlos is going to train Knuckles to be Sammy's understudy!"

Bess giggled. "He'd better train him to like music!" she said.

Nancy shivered with excitement. The lights were dimming and the orchestra began playing. The show was about to begin!

As everyone waited for the curtain to rise,

Nancy turned and whispered to her friends, "The Clue Crew has a lot in common with Francie, you know."

"We do?" Bess asked.

"How?" George asked.

"Because Francie never gives up," Nancy said with a smile. "And neither do we!"

SIGN, PLEASE!
CRAFT YOUR OWN AUTOGRAPH BOOK

What's more fun than collecting autographs from your favorite celebs or theme-park characters? Collecting them in an autograph book you made yourself! It's easy—and sure to stop stars in their tracks!

You'll need:

- Colorful construction paper (about ten pieces)
- Stapler or paper hole-puncher
- Long strand of ribbon or yarn

- Stickers, glitter, photographs, magazine pics, feathers, buttons (or other neat stuff to decorate the cover)
- Crayons or markers
- Glue

Directions:
- Stack papers (the top sheet will be the cover)
- Staple papers together. Or punch holes along the side and tie together with a ribbon or yarn.
- Using crayons or markers, draw pretty pictures or designs on the cover. Or go wild with stickers, glitter, buttons, magazine pics, photographs—anything to make your autograph book totally yours!
- Have fun filling with autographs—or maybe even pawtographs!

Tip: Best friends are the stars of your world. Why not save a page just for them?

Don't miss the next book in the series!

Nancy Drew AND THE CLUE CREW #39

CAROLYN KEENE ILLUSTRATED BY PETER FRANCIS

Museum Mayhem

EIGHT-YEAR-OLD NANCY DREW HELD THE MIRROR in her hand, studying the shape of her right eye. She kept looking at her drawing, then back at her reflection. She wanted to get it just right. "I think my eyes look like bugs . . . ," Nancy said finally.

Her best friend George Fayne leaned over to see. Nancy had a point. Her hair looked the way it did in real life, but her eyes were big ovals with a line down the center. The lashes curled out on both sides, kind of like creepy bug legs.

"A little bit," George said. "The insides look weird. What do you call those things?"

"The pupils!" Miss Alcott said as she walked by. She was carrying a tray of art supplies. There were old coffee cans full of paintbrushes and rolled-up tubes of paint. "You need to fill them out a bit, that's all. Good work, girls."

Nancy looked at her reflection again, then made the pupil a circle instead of a line. Miss Alcott had given her the perfect tip. The circle really did make her eyes look more real.

"Sometimes it seems like she knows everything," Nancy whispered to George.

Bess Marvin stood two easels over. She was hard at work on her self-portrait. Bess was Nancy's other best friend and George's cousin. She loved fashion and design. Whenever they were in art together, Bess was quiet. She would work the entire class and never look up from her drawing.

"My mom told me that Miss Alcott studied in Spain for two years before coming to River Heights Elementary," George said.

"No way," Nancy whispered. "I heard she plays the guitar too. Hannah thought she saw a poster for her band at the music club downtown."

The girls watched their teacher move around the classroom, weaving between easels. She dropped off a few pencils and erasers to different students. Miss Alcott was the coolest teacher to ever come to their school. She had a purple streak in her hair and wore peacock-feather earrings. She was always showing the class famous paintings or drawings. Once she even brought in a collage she had done of New York City—where she grew up. The buildings were made out of newspaper and scraps of glittery fabric, which made them sparkle. Nancy had never seen a piece of art like that before.

Sydney Decker, a student at the easel beside them, seemed to be listening to their conversation. Sydney was supersmart. She always got As on her science tests and math tests, even when everyone else failed. "I heard she traveled all around Peru," Sydney chimed in. "She told Jess Ramos that she got her bag in Lima."

"Lima?" George asked. "Like the bean?"

"No, silly," Sydney said. "Lima—the capital of Peru. You know, Machu Picchu?"

Nancy and George shared a look. They had heard of Peru before, but sometimes it felt like Sydney was speaking another language.

Geography was one of her favorite subjects, so she always talked about different countries. Sometimes they would catch her looking at maps in computer class.

Robby Parsons looked up from his drawing. He wasn't very good at art, so his pictures always ended up a bit strange. His nose looked like a mushroom. His eyes were two different shapes and sizes. Miss Alcott liked to call his drawings "abstract."

"Do you know where she lives?" Robby asked. "It has to be somewhere cool."

"She lives downtown in one of those giant gray buildings," Nancy whispered.

"Yeah," George agreed. "We saw her when we were getting ice cream at the Scoop. She was going inside."

"Are you sure?" Robby asked.

Nancy almost laughed at the question. Of course she and George were sure. Together with Bess, they formed the Clue Crew. They were always searching for clues and were pretty good detectives. They helped solve mysteries around River

Heights. Sometimes it was a stolen wallet or cell phone. Other times it was more serious. They'd once helped an old lady find a missing puppy.

"Definitely," Nancy answered Robby. "She was carrying two bags of groceries."

As Robby went back to his drawing, Miss Alcott set down the last of the art supplies on her desk. She glanced up at the clock. "We only have a few more minutes, so finish up your self-portraits," she said. "And I want to remind everyone about our field trip on Friday."

At the words "field trip," the entire class erupted in cheers. "Par-ty! Par-ty!" Robby chanted. His best friend, Kevin Lim, let out a few loud hoots.

"It's not a party. . . ." Miss Alcott laughed. "Though I promise we'll have a lot of fun. As all of you know, the Simon Cross Art Institute has agreed to let us tour and sleep over at the museum. We'll spend the night in their medieval armor wing."

"Do we have to bring tents?" Amelia Davis asked.

"Just your sleeping bag and pillow," Miss Alcott said. "And anything else you need to be comfortable."

"Like your teddy bear." Kevin laughed. Amelia shot him a dirty look.

"Those armor dudes are scary!" Robby yelled. "I went there a few years ago, and they all had these giant swords."

"What will we do there?" George asked.

"At the museum, we'll go on a tour and eat at the restaurant. We'll draw and paint in the classrooms. There are so many incredible works of art there. I can't wait to show you the impressionist wing. They even have an early Monet." Miss Alcott looked so happy as she described it, even if the rest of the class wasn't sure exactly which artist she was talking about. They'd only had art class for a few weeks. It was hard to remember all the different names.

As the class ended, Miss Alcott went around the room again, collecting stray pencils and mirrors. "Make sure you get your permission slips to me by Thursday at the latest," she said.

"You'll need them for the trip. Great job, Bess," she added as she passed Bess's drawing.

"You have to let us see," George said. She leaned over, trying to get a better look.

Bess pulled it away. "One minute. I have to fix my lips."

Nancy and George waited impatiently, ready to see the secret drawing Bess had been hiding from them the entire class.

"Come on Bess! We're dying to see it," Nancy cried.

Finally, Bess spun her sketch pad around, revealing the picture she'd been working on. The girl in the drawing had the same eyes as Bess. She had the same thick bangs and light shoulder-length hair. She even had the same way of smiling that Bess did.

"That's amazing!" George said. "The drawing looks exactly like you."

Bess's cheeks turned pink. "Thanks. So . . . what did I miss?"

Nancy and George laughed. "Are you serious? You didn't hear anything Miss Alcott said?"

Bess shrugged. "I guess I was really concentrating. . . ."

"She reminded us about the field trip on Friday. Don't forget your permission slip," Nancy said. She grabbed her backpack and headed for the door with George. Bess tucked her sketch pad in her cubby, then followed behind them.

"How could I forget? I've been excited for the last two weeks. Did you know that the Simon Cross Art Institute has a two-story mural in it? Or this room where you can throw paint on the walls?"

"That's crazy," Nancy said.

"It's a special exhibit!" Bess said.

"I've been saving my allowance," George said. "I want to get something cool from the gift shop."

The girls huddled together in the hallway. Nancy was smiling so much her face hurt. Field trips at River Heights were always so much fun, and now they were going to have one with their favorite teacher. "Dinner with Miss Alcott, a sleepover with all our friends . . . what could be better than this?"

NANCY DREW AND THE CLUE CREW®
Test your detective skills with more Clue Crew cases!

FROM ALADDIN • PUBLISHED BY SIMON & SCHUSTER

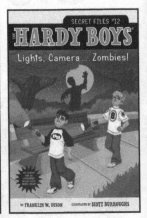

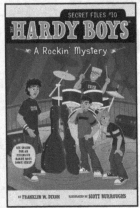

Nancy Drew: Ghost of Thornton Hall

SOME FAMILIES KEEP DEADLY SECRETS!

Jessalyn Thornton's fateful sleepover at the abandoned Thornton estate was supposed to be a pre-wedding celebration, but the fun ended when she disappeared. While her family searches for clues, others refuse to speak about the estate's dark past. Did something supernatural happen to Jessalyn, or is someone in Thornton Hall holding something besides family secrets?

dare to play.

WHEN YOU'RE A KID, THE MYSTERIES ARE JUST THAT MUCH BIGGER . . .
NANCY DREW AND THE CLUE CREW
#2
SECRET SAND SLEUTHS
All-new comics from
PAPERCUTZ™!